# Thunder Creek Ranch

## Sonya
Spreen Bates

Illustrated by
Kasia Charko

ORCA BOOK PUBLISHERS

*For Riley, who agreed to be Tommy for the big jump.*

Text copyright © 2013 Sonya Spreen Bates
Illustrations copyright © 2013 Kasia Charko

**Library and Archives Canada Cataloguing in Publication**

Bates, Sonya Spreen
Thunder Creek ranch / Sonya Spreen Bates ; illustrated by Kasia Charko.
(Orca echoes)

Issued also in electronic formats.
ISBN 978-1-4598-0112-7

I. Charko, Kasia, 1949- II. Title. III. Series: Orca echoes
PS8603.A8486T58 2013          jc813'.6          C2012-907495-0

First published in the United States, 2013
**Library of Congress Control Number**: 2012952960

**Summary**: Jake and Tommy are about to learn why their grandparents' farm
is called Thunder Creek Ranch.

Orca Book Publishers gratefully acknowledges the support for its publishing programs
provided by the following agencies: the Government of Canada through the Canada Book
Fund and the Canada Council for the Arts, and the Province of British Columbia
through the BC Arts Council and the Book Publishing Tax Credit.

MIX
Paper from
responsible sources
**FSC** **FSC® C004071**
www.fsc.org

ANCIENT FOREST ™
FRIENDLY

*Orca Book Publishers is dedicated to preserving the environment and has printed
this book on Forest Stewardship Council® certified paper.*

Cover artwork and interior illustrations by Kasia Charko
ORCA BOOK PUBLISHERS          ORCA BOOK PUBLISHERS
PO Box 5626, Stn. B                    PO Box 468
Victoria, BC Canada                    Custer, WA USA
v8R 6s4                                        98240-0468

www.orcabook.com
Printed and bound in Canada.

16  15  14  13  •  4  3  2  1

## Chapter One
# THE LOOKOUT

Jake grabbed the branch above him and climbed higher into the tree. It was the tallest tree on Grandpa's farm. From the top, he could see right across the valley. He pulled out his binoculars and peered through the lenses.

*I am the lookout on a tall ship*, he thought. *We have been at sea for many weeks. Our supplies are low. I search for land.*

"I need a boost, Jake," Tommy called from the ground.

Jake glanced down at his little brother, hopping up and down as he tried to grab on to the lowest branch.

He had just had his eighth birthday, but he was still as shrimpy and hopeless as ever.

*The crew is restless,* Jake thought, looking through the binoculars again. *We must find land soon or perish.*

A cool breeze blew the hair off his forehead. Jake tried to imagine that the rich brown soil was a deep blue ocean and that the sparrows flying overhead were seagulls. It wasn't easy. He could hear Grandpa's tractor rumbling away in the next field, and the herd of cows looked nothing like a pod of dolphins. He turned the binoculars toward the neighbor's house.

"Land ho!" he cried.

"What land?" asked Tommy. "Help me up, Jake. I can't see anything down here."

"Just wait," said Jake. "You can have a turn in a minute."

Tommy was always bugging him, asking for help or tagging along when he wasn't wanted. Jake had tried to sneak out of the house without him, but Grandma had insisted Tommy come too. "It's a big place,"

she had said. "You stick together." Jake sighed. He wished there was someone else to hang out with. Last Christmas his cousin Lexie had gone skiing with them and they'd had lots of fun, even if she did think she knew everything.

Someone came out of the house on the neighbor's farm. The person was quite short, bundled up in a jacket that looked too big for them. Jake squinted into the binoculars. He thought it would be old Ned McNash, but it wasn't. This person didn't even have gray hair.

"What's going on?" asked Tommy. "What can you see?"

"There's a kid over at the McNash place," said Jake.

"A kid?" said Tommy. "What's a kid doing over there?"

"I don't know," said Jake. He leaned forward to get a better look and almost fell out of the tree. "He's going out to the barn."

Jake stared through the binoculars. Ned and Mildred McNash had lived on the farm next door to Grandma and Grandpa ever since Jake could remember. He had never seen anyone visiting, not even the local vet. And never a kid. Could a new family have moved in? Jake hadn't seen a *For Sale* sign out front. Besides, Grandma would have told them if the McNashes were gone. Who could it be?

The kid threw the barn door open and ducked inside. Jake put the binoculars down. "I'm going over there," he said, starting down the tree.

"But we're not supposed to go there," said Tommy. "Mrs. McNash will yell at us again."

"*We* aren't going," said Jake. "*I* am." He jumped off the lowest branch and landed with a thump. "You stay here and keep watch." He handed Tommy the binoculars. "I'll go around the back of the barn. She'll never see me."

"But Grandma told us—" Tommy said.

"I know what Grandma told us," said Jake. "But I'm not going far, and you'll be able to see me the whole time."

Tommy was getting the stubborn look on his face that meant he was going to argue with Jake.

"Look, I'll give you a boost up and you can watch from the lookout," said Jake.

Tommy's face lit up. He had never been to the top of the tree before. Jake cupped his hands for Tommy's foot and boosted him up to the first branch. He watched while Tommy swung his leg over the rough bark.

Tommy grinned down at Jake.

"Be careful," Jake said. "Grandma will kill me if you fall."

"I will," said Tommy.

He started up the tree, and Jake took off across the field toward the McNash farm.

## Chapter Two
# THE NEW NEIGHBOR

Jake ran through the high grass. He hoped there weren't any snakes around. He had seen one sunning itself on a rock near Thunder Creek last summer. But it was still cold. The snow had only just melted, and the snakes would still be hibernating. He hoped.

Reaching the fence, he climbed over and looked toward the McNash house. He hoped Mrs. McNash wasn't looking out the back window. Despite what he had said to Tommy, he didn't want to get her mad. She was like a mother bear protecting her cubs when she got angry.

*I am a soldier, racing across no-man's-land to enemy territory*, he thought. *I must not be seen.* He dashed across the yard and pressed himself against the wall of the barn, breathing hard. There was no sound from the house.

With a sigh of relief, he turned and peered through the barn window. It was dark inside. He cupped his hands around his eyes to keep out the light, but the window was dirty and he still couldn't see anything. *I must complete my scouting mission,* Jake thought. *Information is vital to our battle plans.*

"What are you doing?" said a voice behind him.

Jake spun around. A boy stood before him. He had blond hair and a pudgy face, and he wore a jacket that was two sizes too big for him. He was just a little shorter than Jake.

"Uh, I…" Jake said. "I'm Jake. I live next door—well, my grandparents do. On Thunder Creek Ranch. I saw you go into the barn and thought I'd come over to say hi."

The boy turned to look at Jake's grandparents' house, a small speck on the other side of the field.

"You saw me from there? What were you doing? Spying?"

"No, of course not," said Jake. "I only noticed because there isn't usually anyone around. Where are you from anyway? Did your mom and dad buy this place?"

"Nah, it's my gramp's place," the boy said.

"Oh," said Jake. This was Ned McNash's grandson? Jake hadn't even known he had a kid. "I've never seen you here before."

The boy shrugged. "I've never been here before. We live in Toronto."

"Oh," said Jake again. Toronto sounded like it was a long way away.

"Wanna see the quad bike?" said the boy.

Jake grinned. "Yeah," he said.

It was dark in the barn and smelled like hay and tractor fuel. Tools hung on the walls, and a tractor stood inside the big doors. Tucked in under the ladder to the hayloft was a brand-new quad bike.

"Gramp just bought it," the boy said. He climbed on and put his hands on the handlebars.

"Cool," said Jake. He circled around, admiring it from all angles. His grandparents had an old motorbike they used on the farm, but it was rusted and falling apart. Jake wasn't allowed to touch it.

"Wanna go for a ride?" asked the boy.

Jake looked up to see if he was joking. "Are you allowed to drive it?"

The boy shrugged. He lifted a helmet off a hook on the wall and slid it onto his head. "Mom won't care."

"What about your grandparents?" asked Jake.

"They won't care either. Hop on." The boy scooted forward so there was room on the seat for Jake. He pushed the starter button and the motor roared to life.

Jake watched as the boy pushed the bike back from the wall and turned it toward the door. "Do you know how to drive it?" he asked.

"What's not to know?" the boy said. "Now, are you coming or not?"

Jake hesitated. He had a feeling Mrs. McNash wouldn't like them taking the bike out. But it looked like fun. And it couldn't be any harder than driving a go-cart. He had done that lots of times. He grabbed the other helmet and hopped on the back of the bike.

The boy revved the motor. The bike leapt forward so fast that Jake almost fell off the back. He grabbed on to the boy's jacket, and they sped through the barn doors and into the yard.

## Chapter Three
# THE ANGRY BEAR

The boy drove like a madman. He sped away from the barn, heading straight for the fence. At the last minute he took a hard right, skidding around the corner so close to the wooden planks that Jake could have reached out and touched them. Then he raced across the paddock. The bike flew over the bumps and dips and landed so hard that Jake's teeth chattered. They reached the fence on the other side and careened around the corner again.

"Slow down!" Jake said.

The boy laughed and eased up on the throttle. Then, just when Jake thought he could relax, he cranked up the accelerator again and pulled the bike into a doughnut. Around and around they went, the world spinning by with dizzying speed.

Jake thought he might throw up. "Stop!" he shouted. "Let me off!"

The boy hit the brake. Jake would have gone over the handlebars if the boy hadn't been in front of him. He leapt off and threw his helmet on the ground.

"What's the matter with you? Are you crazy or something?" he shouted.

"What?" said the boy. "I was just having a little fun."

"You call that fun?" said Jake. "You almost killed us."

"Don't be a wuss," the boy said. "A baby could drive this thing and not get hurt. It's a quad bike. You know—four tires on the ground. What could happen?"

Jake glared at him. "How about smashing into the fence or flipping it into a ditch? This isn't a racecourse, you know."

The boy shrugged.

"Jake? Jake?"

Jake turned to see Tommy running across the field toward them. He groaned. Tommy would tell Grandma he had been on the quad bike, and then he would really be in trouble.

"I thought I told you to stay at Grandma and Grandpa's," Jake said when Tommy reached them.

"I did," said Tommy, trying to catch his breath. "But then you went into the barn, and I couldn't see you and Grandma told us—"

"Yeah, I know. Grandma told us to stick together," said Jake, rolling his eyes.

"Who's that?" asked Tommy, glancing at the boy on the bike.

"That's—" Jake realized he didn't know the boy's name.

"I'm Cory," the boy said. He turned the bike off and removed his helmet. "Who are you?"

"Tommy," said Tommy.

"My little brother," said Jake.

Tommy scowled at him. "I'm not that little anymore. I'm eight."

"I'll be nine next month," Cory said. "Want a ride?"

Tommy's eyes grew round. Jake opened his mouth to say, "No way," but the sound of a door slamming made them all stop and look toward the house. Jake saw Mrs. McNash charging across the yard. Her body heaved with every step, and her housecoat flapped behind her in the wind. There was a look of thunder on her face.

"It's Gram," said Cory. "Run!"

Jake didn't need to be told twice. He tore across the paddock and leapt over the fence into Grandpa's field, with Tommy and Cory close behind.

"Cory McNash, you come back here!" shouted Mrs. McNash.

They kept running.

## Chapter Four
# STAMPEDE

They didn't stop until they were two fields away and the house was out of sight.

Jake flopped to the ground, exhausted. "I thought you said you were allowed to ride the quad bike," he said to Cory.

Cory was leaning over to catch his breath. "I didn't think they would care. Mom wouldn't."

"Where did you learn to drive like that anyway?" asked Tommy.

Cory thumped to the ground next to Jake and Tommy. "My dad," he said proudly. "He's a race-car driver."

"Wow, a race-car driver," said Tommy. "That's cool."

"Yeah, way cool," said Jake. He liked to watch car racing on TV. "What kind of cars does he race?"

"Race cars, of course," said Cory.

"Yeah, but what kind?" said Jake. "Formula One? Stock cars? Drag racers?"

Cory looked away. "Uh…all of them," he said.

Jake made a face. "All of them? How can he do that?"

"Well, not at the same time, of course," said Cory. "He drives Formula One the most. And then sometimes he drives a different car. You know, in other races, when there aren't any races for Formula One."

"You're making it up," said Jake.

"I am not!" said Cory. "My dad does drive race cars. At least, he used to." He looked back and forth between the two boys. Obviously they didn't believe him. "He did! And now he owns his own racetrack," he said.

"He owns a racetrack?" said Jake doubtfully.

"You must be rich," said Tommy.

"Well, it's not a really big track," said Cory. "It's a motocross track."

Jake shook his head. Cory was a bragger. "Come on, Tommy," he said. "We better get back to the house. It's almost lunchtime."

He stood and brushed the dirt from his jeans. Looking up, he saw a cow with her calf headed toward them. He frowned. There weren't supposed to be any cows in this field. As he watched, another cow came into view, then another and another.

"Tommy, did you close the gate behind you?" asked Jake.

Tommy stared at the cows. "I was going to, but Cory yelled at me to leave it open for him."

They both turned to look at Cory.

Cory shrugged. "No one told me to close the gate. How was I supposed to know there were cows in there?"

"You always close the gate," Jake said. "Everyone knows that." More and more cows ambled down the slope. There must be twenty of them, all with a calf tagging along. "We have to turn them back," he said. "Grandpa will kill us if he sees them out here."

*I am a ranch hand*, he thought. *I have lost my horse and my dog. But the herd must be returned to home paddock. A storm is brewing.* Jake jumped up and ran toward the cows. He waved his arms and called out, "Get up!" like he had heard his Grandpa do.

The nearest cow lifted her large brown head and turned to look at him. Then she went back to munching the spring grass.

"Come on, help me," Jake yelled at the other two boys.

Tommy walked closer, flapping his arms halfheartedly. "What if they charge me?" he said.

"They won't," said Jake, hoping he was right. Up close, the cows were bigger than he had thought. Almost as big as the bison he had seen at the zoo. "They're used to being herded. Go on! Get back!" he yelled at them.

Jake heard someone laugh.

"Like they're gonna listen to you," said Cory, slouching up behind them.

Jake scowled. "Have you got a better idea?"

Cory shrugged.

"Then help us," said Jake. "You're the one who let them out."

"I guess," said Cory.

The boys spread out and walked toward the cows, waving their arms and calling, "Get up!" and "Get back home!" Jake wished Bella, the sheepdog, were here. She would get them going. Slowly the cows started to turn around.

*The herd is turning,* thought Jake. *And just in time. The storm is upon us. Lightning streaks across the sky. Rain thunders down. We must seek shelter.*

The cows had almost reached the gate when one of the calves bolted. It darted away from the herd and headed in Tommy's direction.

Tommy screamed and ran. The calf kicked up its heels and loped after him.

"Jake! Help!" screamed Tommy.

"Stop running!" called Jake. "It thinks you're playing."

One of the cows turned and trotted toward Jake. It lowered its head as if it might charge. Jake froze. It must be the calf's mother, he thought. He stood still, and the cow lumbered past. Another cow followed, and then another, until the whole herd had started moving. Jake watched helplessly as they streamed past him and disappeared over the rise after Tommy.

## Chapter Five
# CORY TO THE RESCUE

Jake raced to the top of the hill and looked down. Below him, Tommy had reached Thunder Creek. There wasn't much water running. Only a small stream trickled through the wide creek bed. Tommy leapt off a rock, jumped across the stream and continued on into the woods. Most of the herd stopped at the stream for a drink, but the calf leapt neatly across, its mother following.

Jake groaned. How would he ever catch them? Tommy would get lost in the woods. He had never been past Thunder Creek before. Jake had to find him.

Jake took off at a jog down the hill, trying to remember the exact spot where Tommy had entered

the woods. Tommy would stop when he got tired. If Jake could follow his trail, he would find him eventually.

*I am a police tracker,* he thought. *A boy has been kidnapped and taken into the woods. He must be found.*

Just then Jake heard the roar of a motor behind him. He turned. Cory came over the rise on the quad bike.

"I can't believe you took the quad again!" said Jake when Cory reached him. "Mrs. McNash will kill you."

Cory threw the spare helmet at Jake. "You mean she'll kill us. It's the fastest way to find your brother. He could be halfway to Vancouver by now."

Jake glanced toward the woods. The herd was milling about the stream. He couldn't see any sign of Tommy or the two cows that had been following him. Looking up, he noticed dark clouds gathering overhead. It looked like it was going to rain.

Cory was right. The quad bike would be much faster than walking. They had to find Tommy. Jake jammed the helmet on his head.

"All right," he said, climbing on behind Cory. "But take it easy."

"Aye-aye, Captain," said Cory.

Cory took off fast, but Jake was expecting it this time. He held on tight.

"This is Thunder Creek?" asked Cory when they reached the stream. "Why is it called that? It looks more like Dry Creek to me."

"I don't know," said Jake. "Maybe it used to be big. Who cares? We have to find Tommy."

Cory eased the quad bike over the bank of the creek, splashed through the water and then sped up on the other side.

Jake could see trampled grass and broken branches where Tommy and the cows had entered the woods.

*I see signs of the kidnapper,* he thought. *I follow his trail through the forest. He will not escape.*

It was dark in the woods, the light blocked by the leafy canopy above them. Jake had only been in there once before. Grandpa had brought him out to choose

a Christmas tree the previous year. It had looked very different then. Everything was covered with snow, and except for the evergreens, the trees were brown and bare of leaves. Now spring flowers popped up all around them, and the trees were covered in fresh, green growth. It smelled damp and earthy, like the school field after a rain.

"Tommy!" he called. "Tommy!"

There was no answer.

"That way, I think," said Jake, spotting some more broken branches.

Cory steered the quad bike through the trees, following the trail of trampled grass. Jake scanned the forest. He called out every couple of minutes and listened for an answering call. There was no sign of Tommy.

## Chapter Six
# STORM

"He's got to be here somewhere," said Cory.

They had lost the trail. But in a small clearing they found the cow and her calf grazing on the fresh, green grass. The calf startled at the sight of the quad bike, and the two animals trotted back the way they had come. Tommy was nowhere in sight.

Jake hopped off the quad.

"Tommy!" he called for what seemed like the thousandth time. "Tommy!"

He couldn't tell which way Tommy had run. The grass had been trampled by the cows and then flattened even more by the quad.

Overhead, the sky had filled with roiling clouds. Jake heard the rumble of thunder in the distance. A storm was coming.

"Tommy's probably hiding," said Jake. "He hates thunderstorms."

"What a baby," said Cory.

"He's not a baby," said Jake. "He's the same age as you."

"I'm almost nine," said Cory. "And I'm not a scaredy-cat like him."

"He's not a scaredy-cat," said Jake.

"He's scared of cows and thunderstorms," said Cory. "He's even scared of my gram. Is there anything he's not scared of?"

"Yeah, plenty," said Jake, getting angry. "He outran a cougar last Christmas."

"Little baby Tommy?" said Cory. "I doubt it."

"He did too!" said Jake. "Ask anyone."

"I will," said Cory.

The two boys glared at each other. Jake wanted to say more, but he felt a bit guilty. He had called Tommy a baby once too. And a wuss. The truth was, Tommy *was* a bit of a scaredy-cat. But Jake wasn't going to let Cory McNash call him that.

Lightning flashed overhead, and a clap of thunder boomed all around them. The boys jumped.

"Take cover," said Jake. He darted for a clump of low bushes. Cory revved the quad bike and accelerated into the trees. Rain started falling in big heavy drops.

"Get off the quad!" yelled Jake. "Lightning is attracted to metal."

"Aahhh!" Cory jumped off the quad as if it had already been struck by lightning. He dashed over to a big tree and crouched below it.

"Stay away from tall trees too!" said Jake.

Cory leapt up again and ran to a different tree. He looked up to see how tall it was, changed his mind and darted toward a third tree. At the last minute, he changed direction and raced to Jake's side. "I—I'll just stick with you, okay?"

Jake smiled. He took off his helmet and tossed it over by the quad. He didn't know what it was made of, but he wasn't going to take a chance. Cory did the same.

They crouched under the bushes as the storm raged around them. Rain poured down and the wind tore at the tops of the trees. Lightning streaked across the sky. Thunder rumbled so loud, the ground seemed to shake.

Jake wished he knew where Tommy was. He knew Tommy would be scared. He was a bit scared himself. The storm was so loud and fierce. Had Tommy found a safe place to shelter? Or was he out in the open somewhere, exposed to the lightning?

At last the rain slowed and the rumble of thunder grew faint. Jake waited a few more minutes before he and Cory crawled out from the bushes. Cory's hair was plastered to his head, and his face was pale.

"That was some storm," he said with an uneasy laugh. He stamped his feet, his teeth chattering.

Jake thought of saying something about scaredy-cats, but he was too worried about Tommy. He shrugged. "We get them all the time around here," he said. "Mostly in summer though." That's why his grandpa had taught them what to do in a thunderstorm. He hoped Tommy remembered what he had learned. "Tommy!" he called. "Tommy! Where are you?"

"Jake!" Tommy's voice was so faint, Jake wasn't sure he had heard him. "Jake!"

It was definitely Tommy. Jake took off toward the voice.

## Chapter Seven
# ROARING MEG

They found Tommy cowering under the roots of a fallen pine tree.

"Is—is it over?" he said. His hands and knees were covered in mud. Under the smear of dirt, his face was pale.

"Yeah, it's gone," said Jake.

Tommy breathed a sigh of relief. "I found a hiding spot and made myself as small as I could," he said. "Just like Grandpa told us."

"That's good," said Jake. He put a hand on Tommy's shoulder and gave it a squeeze. He was feeling relieved himself.

"Let's get out of here," said Cory. "I'm freezing."

Jake was cold too. He was soaked to the skin, and the wind felt like ice. Even his socks were squelching in his sneakers. He led the way back to where they had left the quad. There wasn't room for three of them on the seat, so he tossed the spare helmet to Tommy.

"You can ride with Cory, if you want," he said. He glared at Cory with a look that said, *Go slow or else.*

Tommy's face lit up. "Really?"

"Sure. Hop on," said Cory.

"All right!" said Tommy. He jumped on behind Cory and clung to Cory's sides, his legs dangling.

Jake walked in front of the quad to make sure Cory didn't do anything stupid. He followed the trail of flattened grass. It wound around trees and rocks and seemed to be going in circles. He was sure there was a quicker way back to Grandma and Grandpa's house, but he didn't know exactly in which direction the house was. He didn't want to get lost.

*I have found the lost boy,* he thought. *I lead the team back to home base. Our search has been successful. The boy has been saved.*

At last they approached Thunder Creek. The first thing he noticed was that the cows were gone. He groaned. They would have no hope of finding them now. They would have to tell Grandpa that they had let them out.

Then, as they got closer, he noticed something else. Thunder Creek was no longer a trickle. The storm had made the water rise. It wasn't a tiny little stream anymore. A stream of water as wide as the lane leading to Grandpa's farm rushed down the creek bed. It lapped at the rocky edges and frothed and swirled and bubbled like the sea in a storm. Water sprayed in a fine mist onto Jake's face. He could hear rocks tumbling below the surface.

Jake remembered his grandmother saying something about "Roaring Meg" coming to Thunder

Creek with the spring storms. He hadn't known what she meant at the time. The storm had changed the creek from a quiet trickle to a roaring monster as quick as a flash. It really was Thunder Creek.

"Oh no!" said Tommy. "How are we going to get across?"

It was exactly what Jake was thinking. There was no way they could take the quad across. The water was too deep. The creek was too wide to jump over, and they couldn't wade through it either. They would be swept away. The water was running too fast.

"What are we gonna do, Jake?" said Tommy, hopping off the bike.

"Don't worry," said Jake. "We'll figure something out."

Cory turned the quad off. "Gram's gonna kill me," he muttered.

"Why don't we get some stuff from the woods and make a bridge?" said Tommy.

Jake glanced back at the trees. "I don't know. We could try." He remembered doing something like that at school camp. But they'd had wood of just the right size—and ropes.

"That'll never work," said Cory. "What a stupid idea."

Tommy looked crushed.

"It's not a stupid idea," said Jake. "Have you got a better one?"

Cory looked away sullenly.

"I didn't think so. Let's go get some branches then," said Jake.

## Chapter Eight
# THE BIG JUMP

They searched for half an hour, dragging branches to the creek and heaving them into position.

*I am a pioneer*, thought Jake. *We are searching for good farmland. We will not survive in the forest. We must reach the other side of the river.*

Most of the branches were too short and got swept away by the raging water. Only two were long enough. The first branch was thick and sturdy, but it was too heavy to lift into position. It tumbled into the creek, almost taking Tommy in with it. The second was long and spindly and cracked as soon as Jake put his weight on it.

"This isn't going to work," said Jake, scrambling back from the edge.

"I told you it was a dumb idea," said Cory.

"It wasn't," said Tommy. "It would have worked if the creek wasn't so wide."

"If the creek wasn't so wide, we wouldn't need a bridge, stupid," said Cory. "We'd just jump across."

Tommy's face crumpled. He looked like he might cry.

Jake glared at Cory. It wasn't Tommy's fault that they were stuck on the wrong side of the creek. He didn't ask the calf to chase him. And he hadn't made the storm come. It wasn't Tommy's fault the creek was so wide and the water so fast. Then Jake had an idea. "Hold on a sec," he said. "You might be on to something."

"What?" asked Cory.

Tommy looked up expectantly.

"If the creek wasn't so wide, we could jump across," said Jake.

"Yeah, so?" said Cory. "You got some magic that's gonna shrink it?"

"Don't be stupid," said Jake. "Up near the top field, there's a gully the creek runs through. It's not very wide. I bet we could jump that. It's worth a try."

"What about the quad?" asked Cory.

Jake shook his head. "We'll have to leave the quad here. It's too steep and rocky up there. We'd never get it across, not even when the creek goes down."

Cory scowled, but he followed them upstream toward the top field. It was rough going. The creek led them into the woods where the bushes grew close to the bank. The ground grew steep, strewn with rocks and boulders. At last they scrambled up a knoll and onto a rock platform at the edge of a small gully. The creek raced through the narrow gap, splashing and foaming an arm's length or more below them. Jake looked across to the other side. It wasn't as close as he remembered. It had to be at least as wide as a picnic table, maybe wider. Could they jump across?

"I think I could jump that," said Tommy, looking down at the swiftly moving water. "Remember when I won the long-jump competition at Sports Day?"

Tommy was a good jumper. And Jake was pretty sure he could make it. But in long jump, there wasn't a raging creek below them, waiting to swallow them up if they missed.

"I think I could make it too," Jake said. "What about you, Cory?"

Cory was standing well away from the edge. "Yeah, sure," he said. "No sweat." He didn't look so sure though.

"Do you want to try a couple of practice jumps first?" asked Jake.

Cory frowned at him. "What for? If you two can do it, I can."

"Okay," said Jake. He glanced at Tommy. "I'll go first."

Tommy nodded.

Jake scuffed at the edge of the rock. It dropped steeply into the gully. The rain had made it wet and slippery. He would have to be careful. He moved away from the edge to give himself a good run-up.

*I am an Olympic long-jump champion,* he thought. *I am going out for a practice jump. I've done it hundreds of times before.*

He focused on a spot on the other side. That was where he would land. He took a deep breath and then sprinted for the edge. Three strides, four, five. His foot hit the edge and he took a mighty leap. From the corner of his eye he saw the foaming white water flash by below. He landed with a thump on the rock and tumbled to the ground. He was so relieved, he almost laughed out loud.

"Okay, your turn, Tommy," he said, scrambling to his feet.

Tommy looked worried, but he backed up to where Jake had started.

"Is it slippery?" he asked.

"It's not too bad," said Jake. "Just don't look down."

"What if I don't make it?" said Tommy.

"You will," said Jake. "You can jump farther than me, and I made it."

"You're right," said Tommy. "I can do it." He frowned in concentration. "I can do it."

Jake was almost afraid to look as Tommy started running toward the edge. Closer and closer he ran.

"Come on, Tommy," Jake muttered.

Tommy took off from the edge. His arms windmilled as he flew across the gap. He landed perfectly, a good foot beyond where Jake had landed.

"I did it!" cried Tommy.

"You did it!" said Jake. He slapped Tommy on the back, grinning like a baboon.

They both turned back to look at Cory.

"All right, Cory," said Jake. "Your turn."

## Chapter Nine
# A CLOSE CALL

Cory looked scared. He shuffled closer to the edge of the gully and looked down.

"You don't have to jump if you don't want to," said Jake. "We could go and get Grandpa."

Cory stepped back and glared at Jake. "Don't you think I can do it?"

"That's not what I meant," said Jake. "I meant if you don't want to…if you're a bit nervous or something—"

"Are you calling me chicken?" asked Cory.

Jake shrugged. "I didn't say that."

"'Cause I'm not," said Cory. "I can jump that easy."

"Bet you can't," said Tommy.

"Can too," said Cory.

"So prove it," said Tommy. "Go ahead, jump."

"All right, I will," said Cory. He stomped back to where Jake and Tommy had started their runs.

Jake watched nervously. Cory's mouth was a grim line. He clenched his fists and unclenched them. He seemed to be waiting for the right moment, as if a change in the wind might help him.

"Go on. What are you waiting for?" asked Tommy.

Jake shushed him. He wasn't sure Cory could make the jump. He didn't look very athletic, and he had been breathing hard as they climbed the hill to the gully. Maybe he didn't do anything besides riding trail bikes. Maybe he had never tried a long jump before.

Cory started running. He looked angry, and he charged toward the edge as if he were a bull. Three steps, four. Jake held his breath as Cory took off. Cory's foot slipped as he pushed off, and he threw his arms in the air. His legs moved back and forth like he was still running. Jake gasped. He wasn't going to make it.

Cory's foot hit the edge of the bank and skidded out from under him. He landed on his stomach, draped across the rock, and started sliding.

"Help!" Cory screamed.

Jake and Tommy leapt forward and grabbed Cory's hands.

Cory was heavy. And the rock was wet and slippery. Jake felt himself being pulled closer and closer to the edge.

"Pull!" he said to Tommy.

"I am," said Tommy.

Cory wriggled like a fish on a line, trying to get his feet on the rock. He glanced fearfully at the water lapping at his heels.

"Help! I can't swim," he cried.

Jake braced his foot on a nearby bush. He leaned back and pulled with all his strength.

"We've got you. Pull yourself up!" he said.

Cory jammed his feet against the rock. Jake and Tommy pulled and slowly Cory inched upward.

Jake got a better grip and heaved. Within seconds the three of them were panting in a jumbled heap on the edge of the rock.

"Wow, that was close," said Tommy, rolling away from them. "You almost fell into the creek. We would never have gotten you out. You would have been swept away like the branches were."

Cory climbed to his feet. His face was pale. He looked down into the water again and stepped away from the edge. He shrugged. "No biggie. We made it. Let's get out of here."

"You could at least say thanks," said Jake.

Cory glanced at him. Jake could see he was still shaken. He just didn't want to admit it. "Yeah, thanks," he said. "Now let's go."

They found a track a little ways downstream. Jake recognized it as the one Grandpa had followed to get to the gully. The track took them down through the forest and into the field behind the house.

"Grandma? Grandpa?" Jake said as they burst in through the back door.

Grandma leapt up from the table. She looked like she had been crying. "Jake! Tommy! Thank goodness you're safe." She wrapped her arms around them in a bear hug. "Where have you been? We've been so worried."

"I got chased by a bull, Grandma," said Tommy. "And then I got lost in the woods and the storm came. I made myself really small, just like you and Grandpa always say to do."

Jake rolled his eyes. "It was a calf," he said. "But we did get caught in the storm. The creek rose, and we couldn't get across."

"Roaring Meg," said Grandma, shaking her head. "She's come early this year. So how did you get home?"

"We crossed at the gully," said Jake.

"And I made the biggest jump," said Tommy. "Even bigger than Jake's, and Cory—"

"Cory made it over too," said Jake quickly, frowning at Tommy. "But we have to tell you something, Grandma."

He swallowed. "We let the cows out. The ones in the home field. We didn't mean to. We tried to get them back, but then a calf started chasing Tommy and we… we lost them." He looked down at his feet. He didn't want to see the anger in Grandma's face.

Grandma laughed. "Is that what you're worried about?" she asked. Jake looked up. "Those cows came home hours ago. They know when a storm is coming, even if you don't. Now I better call the McNashes and let them know you're home safe. They've been worried sick about Cory."

"Grandma?" asked Tommy before she could go. "Are you sure all the cows got home? Even the one that chased me across the creek? It might be stuck on the other side. I don't think it could jump across like we did."

"Yes, Tommy," said Grandma. She smiled and ruffled his hair. "They all came home before the storm. Even the little rascal that chased you."

She went to find the phone. Jake, Tommy and Cory were left staring at each other. They were wet and covered in mud, and Cory had a scratch down one side of his face. Jake was almost as exhausted as he had been when they'd gotten stranded on Wildcat Run. Then Tommy's stomach gave a ferocious growl, and they all burst out laughing.

"I gotta go," said Cory with a grin. "See you guys tomorrow?"

Jake grinned back. "Yeah, see you tomorrow," he said. Cory was a pain. He bragged, drove like a madman and could be kind of mean sometimes. But he wasn't as bad as he tried to be.

"See you tomorrow," said Tommy.

Cory waved and shuffled out the door, letting it bang shut behind him.

"He's cool," said Tommy. "But I'm a better jumper than him, aren't I, Jake?"

"Yeah, you are," said Jake. "Come on. Let's find something to eat."

**Sonya Spreen Bates** is a Canadian writer living in South Australia. Always an avid reader, she was inspired to write children's fiction by her two daughters and their love of the stories she told them. Sonya's stories have been published in Australia, New Zealand and Canada. *Thunder Creek Ranch* is the fourth book about Jake and Tommy in the Orca Echoes series.